The Mischievous Mom at the Art Gallery

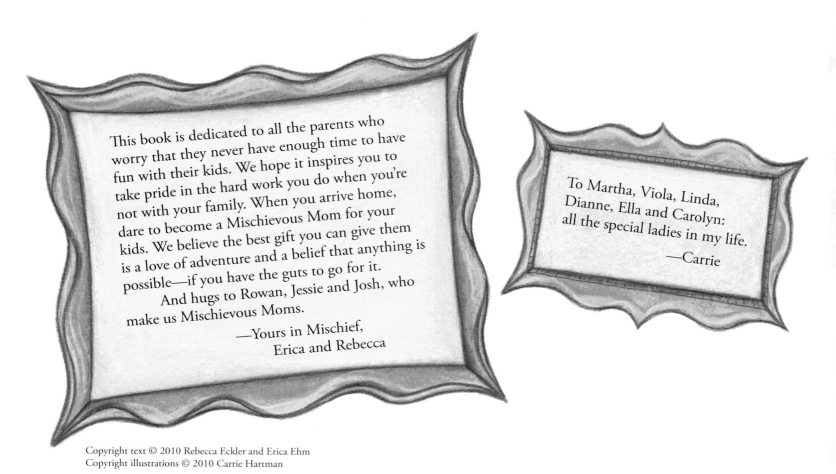

This book is dedicated to all the parents who worry that they never have enough time to have fun with their kids. We hope it inspires you to take pride in the hard work you do when you're not with your family. When you arrive home, dare to become a Mischievous Mom for your kids. We believe the best gift you can give them is a love of adventure and a belief that anything is possible—if you have the guts to go for it.

And hugs to Rowan, Jessie and Josh, who make us Mischievous Moms.

—Yours in Mischief,
Erica and Rebecca

To Martha, Viola, Linda, Dianne, Ella and Carolyn: all the special ladies in my life.

—Carrie

Library and Archives Canada in Publication data available upon request

The Canada Council for the Arts since 1957 | Le Conseil des Arts du Canada depuis 1957

ONTARIO ARTS COUNCIL
CONSEIL DES ARTS DE L'ONTARIO

The publisher gratefully acknowledges the support of the Canada Council for the Arts and the Ontario Arts Council for its publishing program. We acknowledge the support of the Government of Ontario through the Ontario Media Development Corporation's Ontario Book Initiative.

We acknowledge the financial support of the Government of Canada through the Book Publishing Industry Development Program (BPIDP) for our publishing activities.

KPk is an imprint of
Key Porter Books Limited
Six Adelaide Street East, Tenth Floor
Toronto, Ontario
Canada M5C 1H6

Printed and bound in China

10 11 12 13 14 6 5 4 3 2 1

The Mischievous Mom at the Art Gallery

WRITTEN BY
Rebecca Eckler
and Erica Ehm

ILLUSTRATED BY
Carrie Hartman

KPk
Key Porter Kids

It was a typical day for Joshua and Jessie.

They brushed their teeth, got dressed, ate breakfast, and went to school.

They did some writing, practised their reading, and cleaned up after themselves.

They listened to the teachers, shared toys, and ate healthy snacks.

They got on the bus, went back home, and threw down their backpacks.

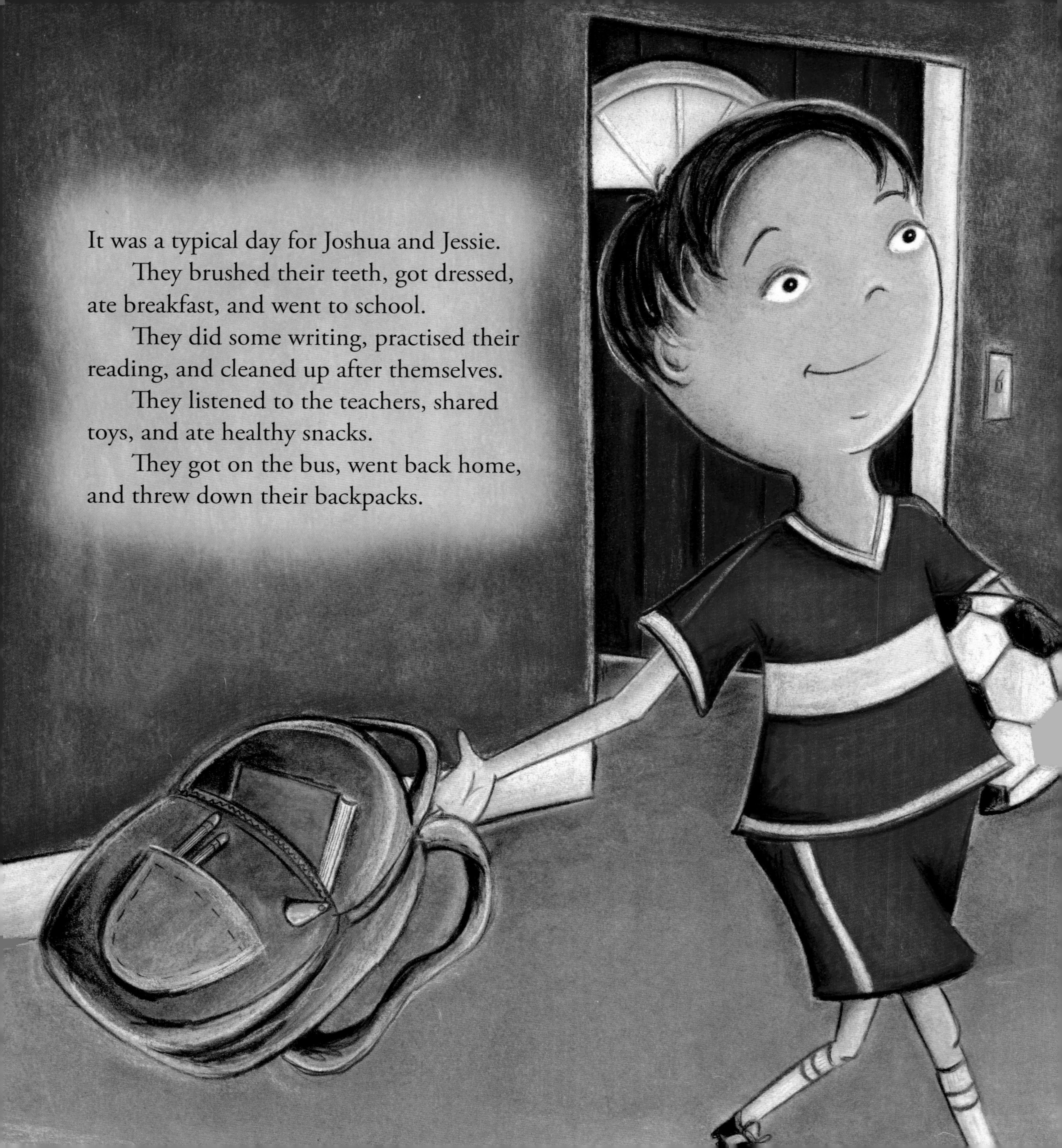
6

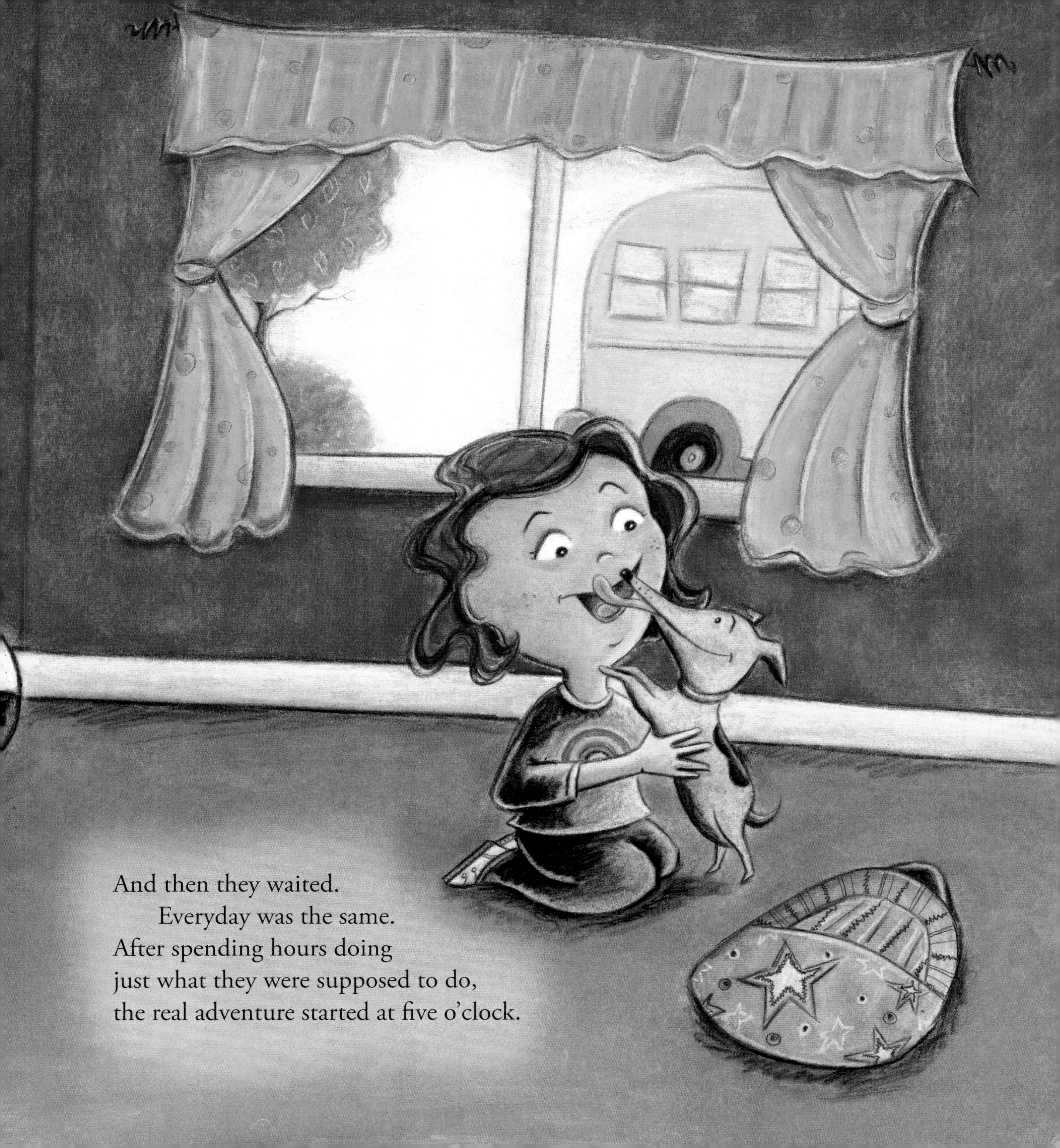

And then they waited.
Everyday was the same.
After spending hours doing
just what they were supposed to do,
the real adventure started at five o'clock.

Five o'clock was when their mom came home from work. And when Mom came home, Joshua and Jessie knew the fun was about to begin. Josh and Jessie's mom was not like them. She was never scared of anything. She loved getting messy. And she was very, very mischievous.

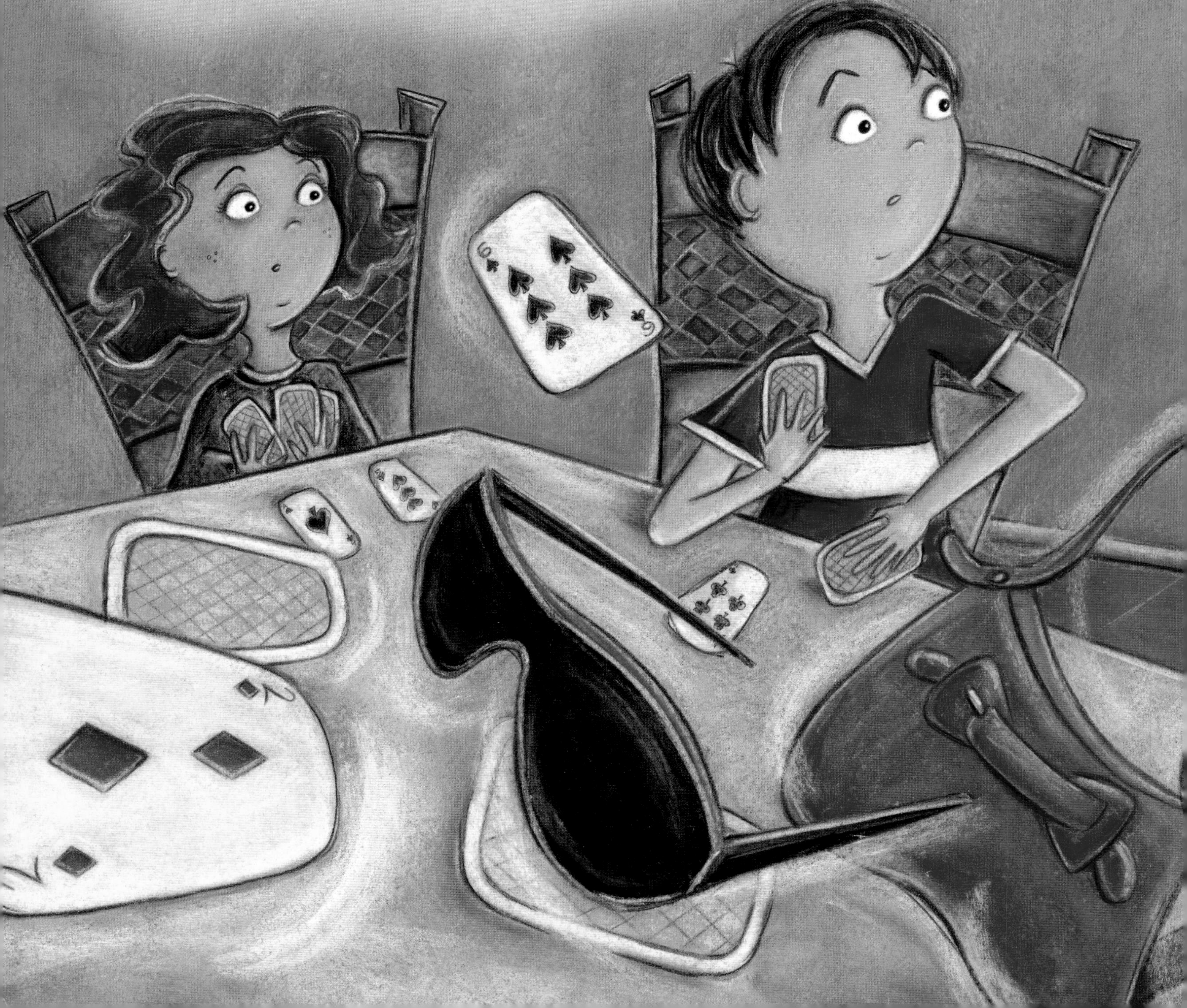

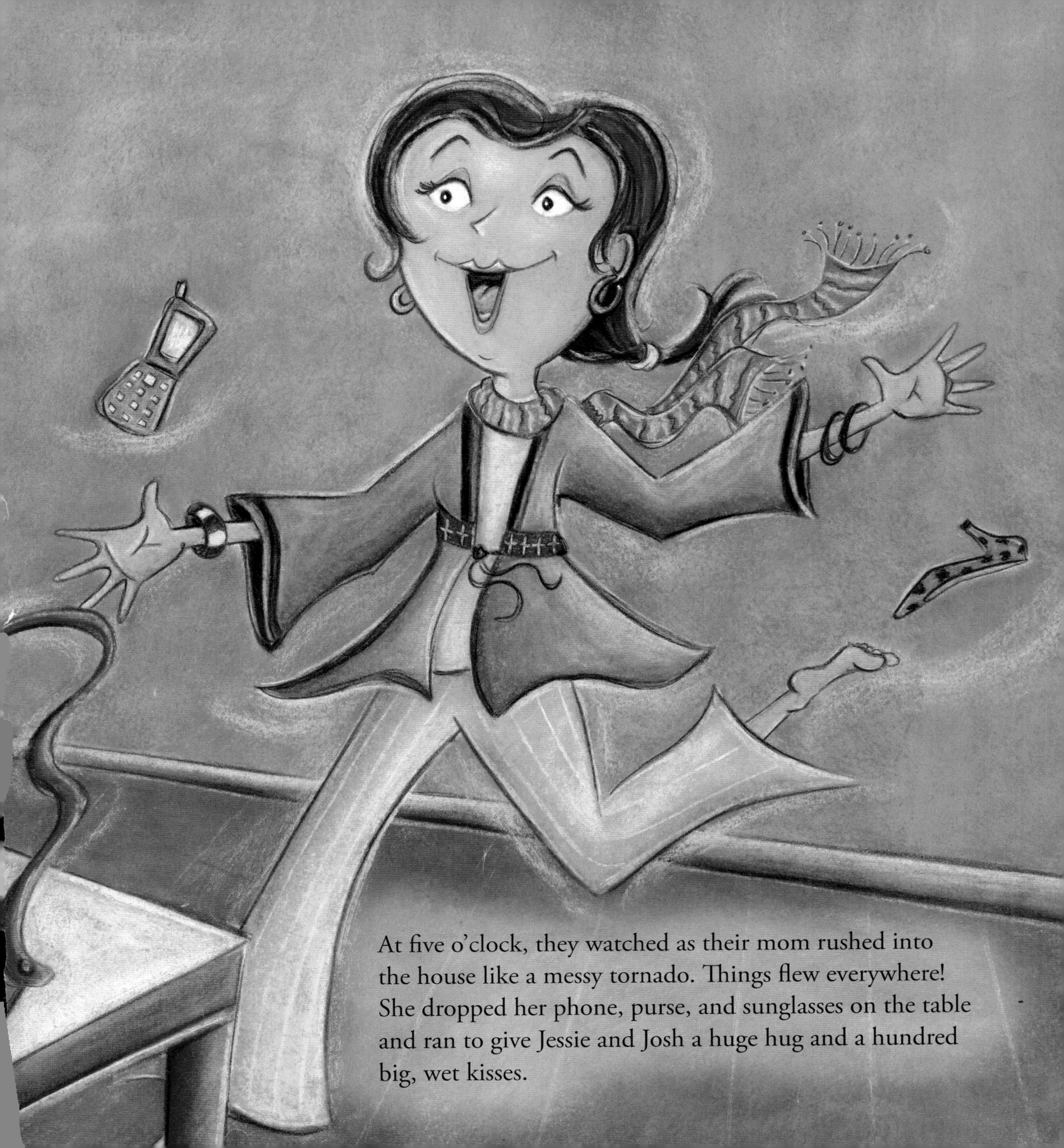

At five o'clock, they watched as their mom rushed into the house like a messy tornado. Things flew everywhere! She dropped her phone, purse, and sunglasses on the table and ran to give Jessie and Josh a huge hug and a hundred big, wet kisses.

"I missed you today!" their mother said. "And I have a surprise!"

Josh and Jessie looked at each other nervously. They knew what that meant.

"A surprise?" they asked slowly. "What is it?"

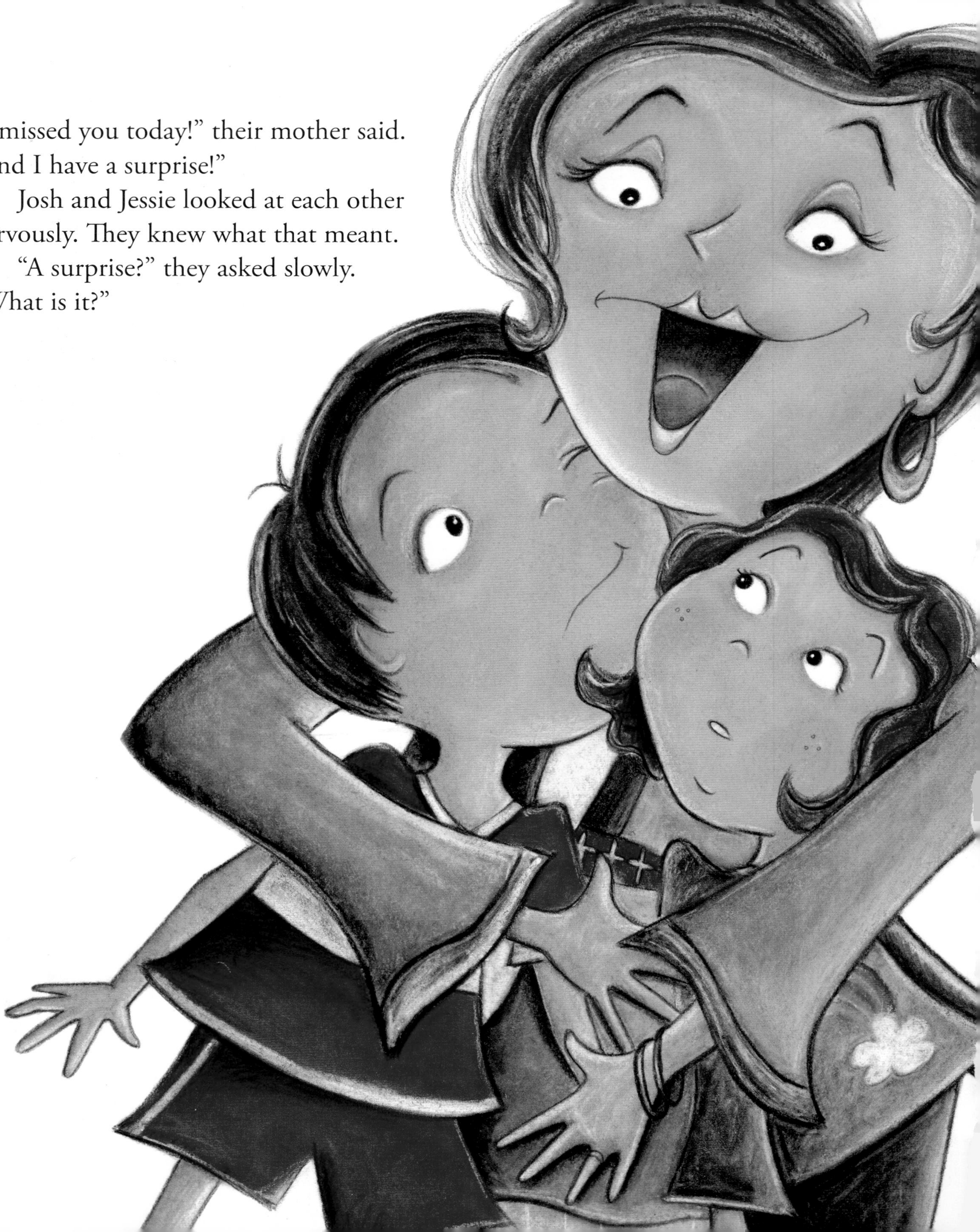

They watched as their mother pulled a big, black envelope with sparkly writing on the front from her purse.

"Guess what?" their mother said. "I've been invited to a very fancy party at the Art Gallery tonight, and there's no one I'd rather go with than the two of you. You are going to be my dates!"

"What are we going to do there?" moaned Jessie. "Art galleries are just for grown-ups."

"Yeah, Mom. What are we going to do at the Art Gallery?" asked Josh.

"Well, I guess we'll stand around and look at the art with all the grown-ups," said Mom. "It'll be fun. I promise!"

But Jessie and Josh didn't think that standing around looking at art, especially with grown-ups, sounded like much fun. It didn't sound like an adventure at all. It sounded b-o-r-i-n-g!

"Now run upstairs and put some party clothes on," said Mom. "And I'll get mine on too!"

You're
You are invited
to the
Art Gallery
7:00 PM
Friday Night

At least their mother's party
clothes were never boring.

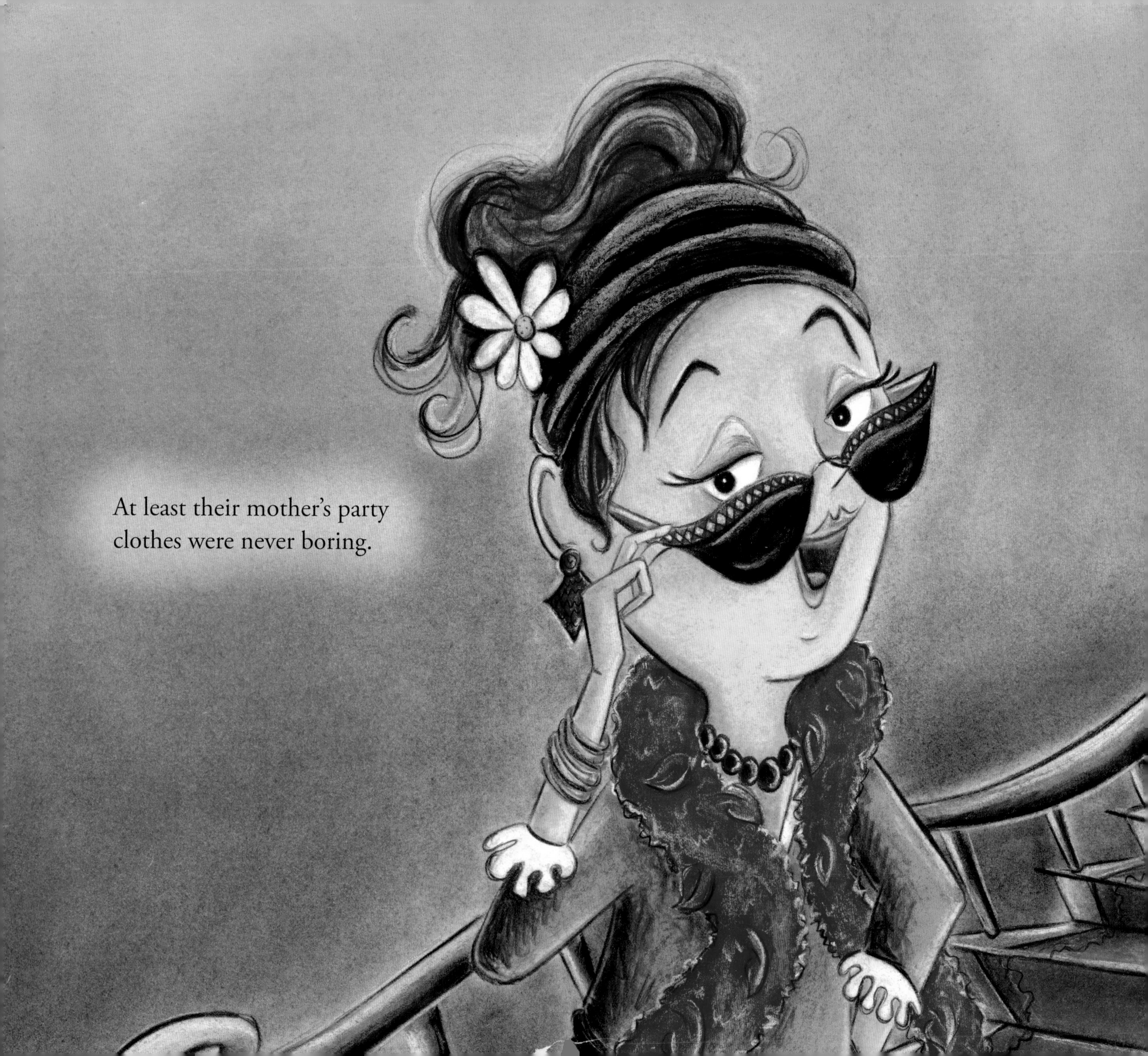

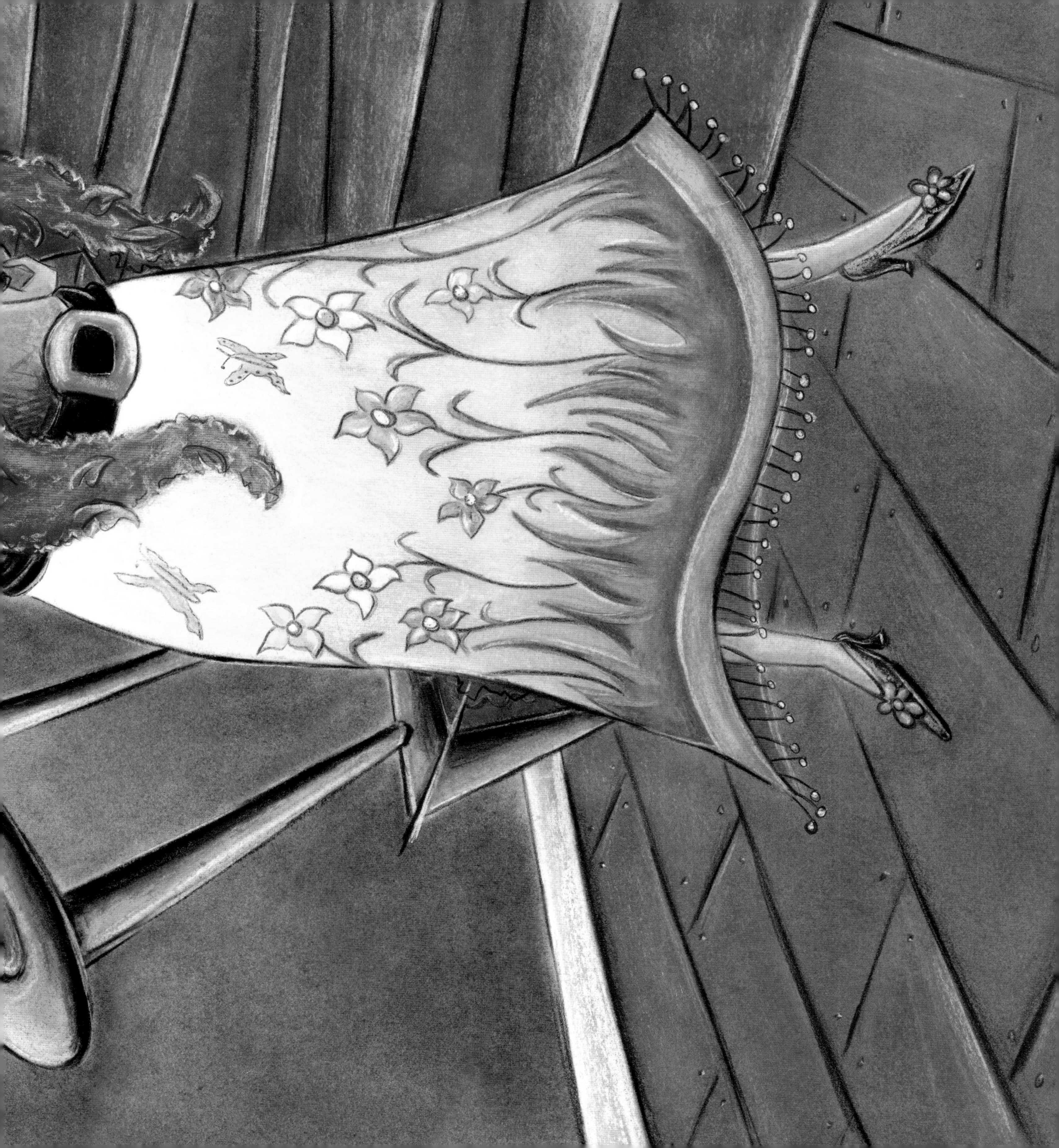

Before leaving the house, Jessie turned to her mother. “Now, Mom,” she said. “Remember, there are probably rules tonight, and as our mother, it’s important that you follow them. I don’t want to get into trouble.”

Josh added, “Do you think you can do that, Mom? Do you think you can follow the rules?”

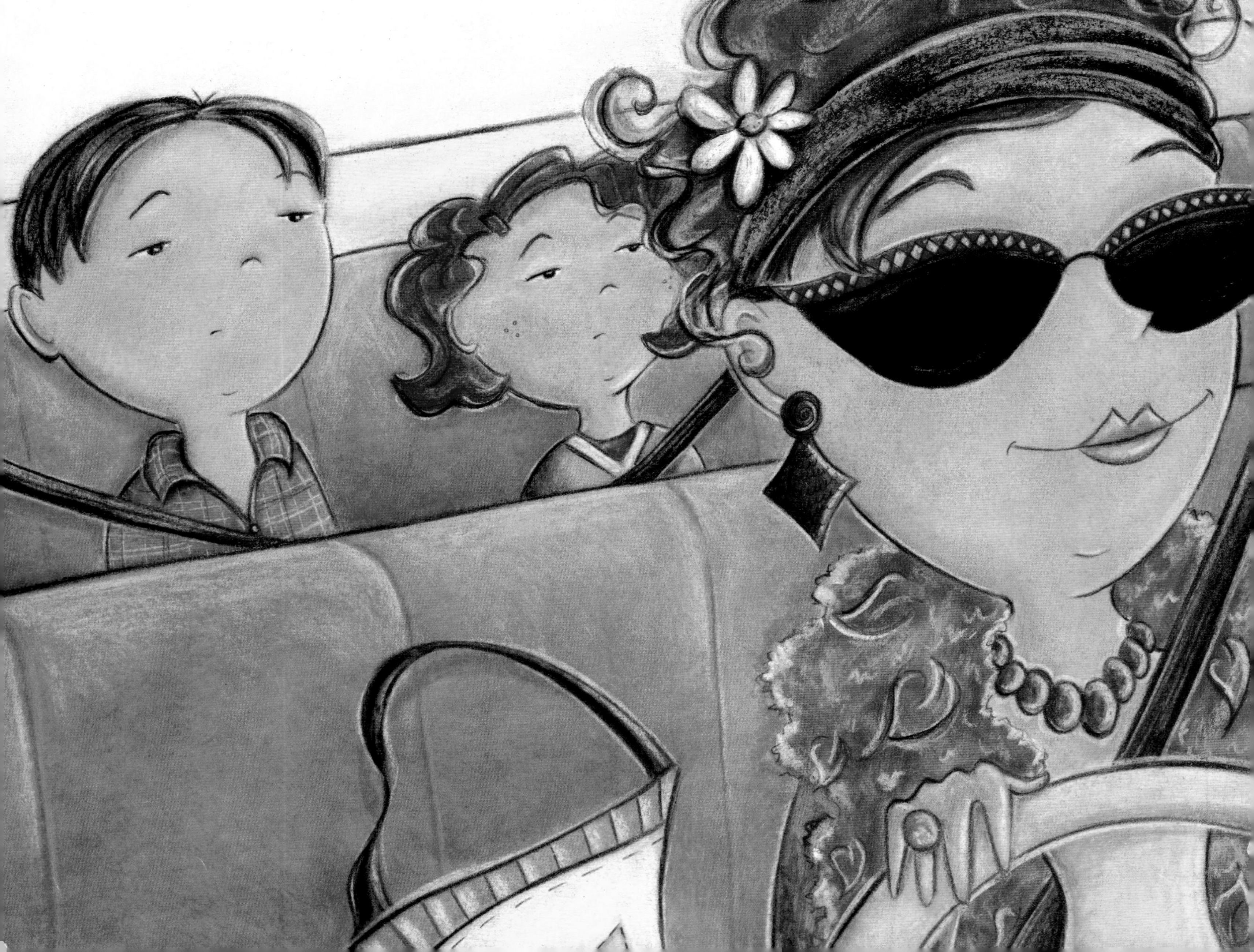

With a mischievous grin, their mom replied, "You know you can count on me to always do the right thing."

"Promise?" they asked.

"I promise!" said their mom, winking her eye.

But Josh and Jessie knew better. They had a Mischievous Mom. She didn't follow rules and she always ended up somewhere she wasn't supposed to be. It was their mom who needed a babysitter, not them. They knew they were going to have to watch out for their mother extra carefully tonight. Who knew what kind of trouble she'd get into?

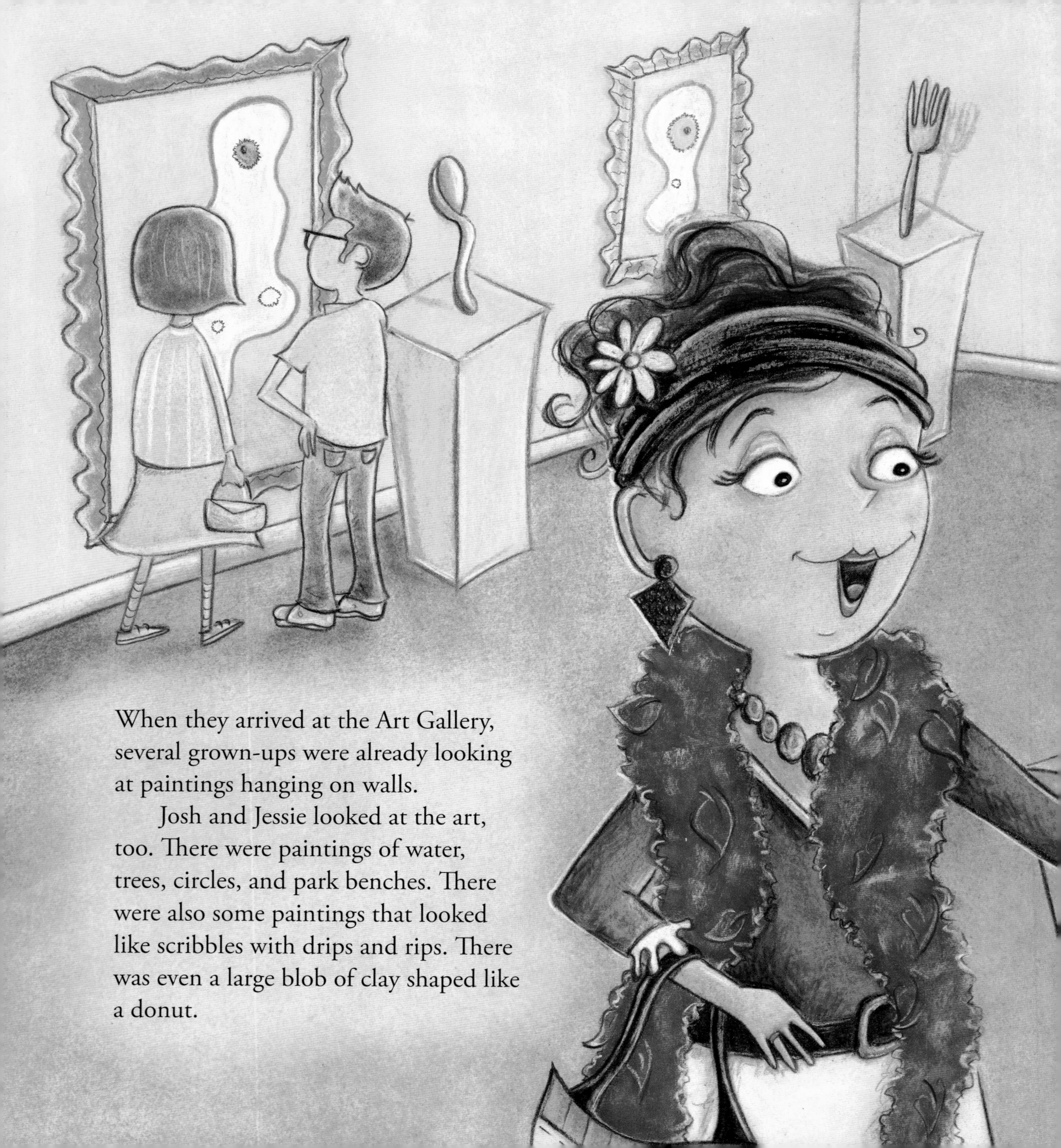

When they arrived at the Art Gallery, several grown-ups were already looking at paintings hanging on walls.

Josh and Jessie looked at the art, too. There were paintings of water, trees, circles, and park benches. There were also some paintings that looked like scribbles with drips and rips. There was even a large blob of clay shaped like a donut.

Josh pointed at it and said, “What is that?”

Mom said, “That’s art!”

Josh looked at Jessie and Jessie looked at Josh. They both looked at the art, trying to see what their mother saw. Josh whispered in Jessie’s ear, “We could do that in our sleep!” Jessie whispered back, “Yeah, I did that when I was three!”

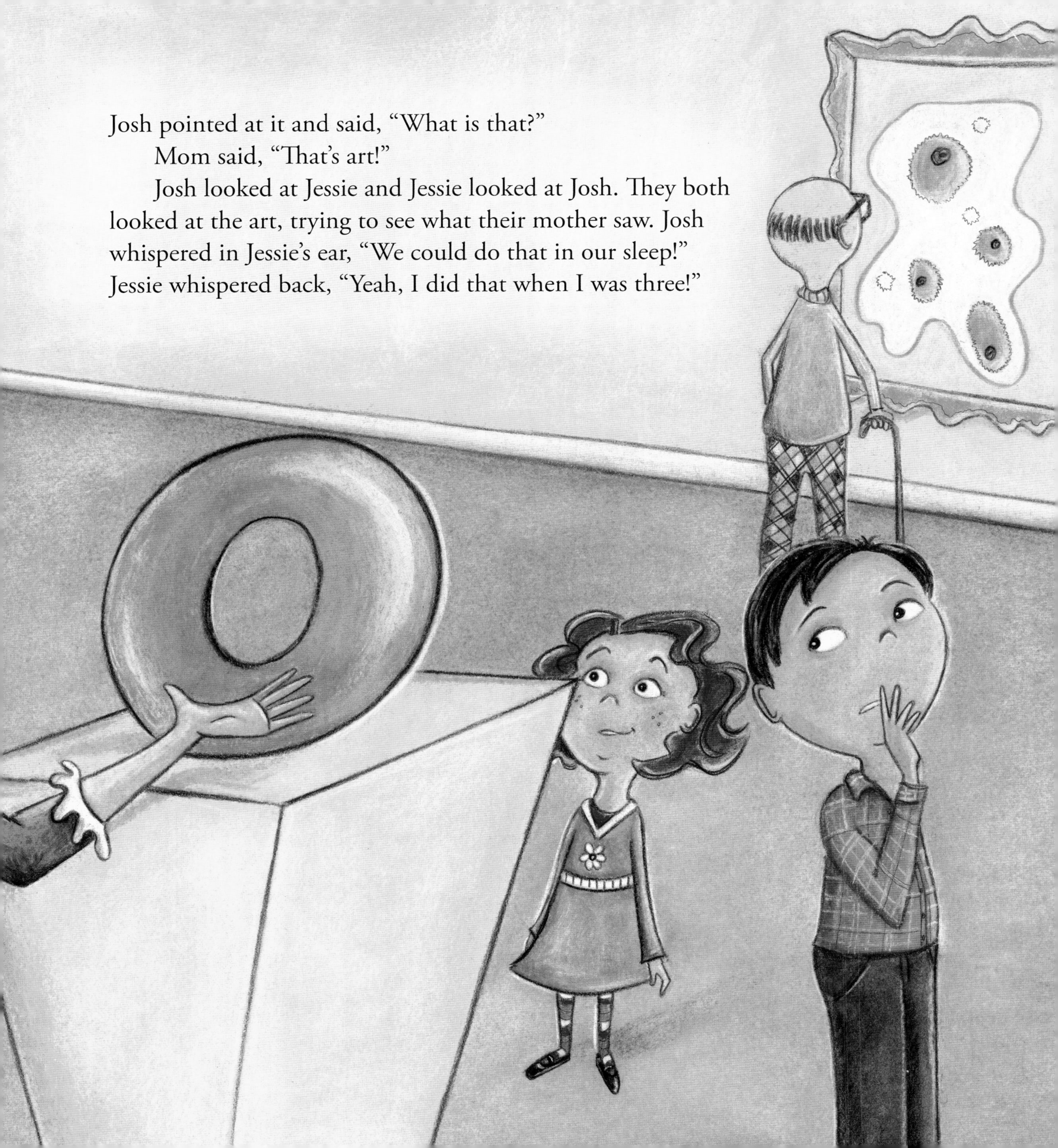

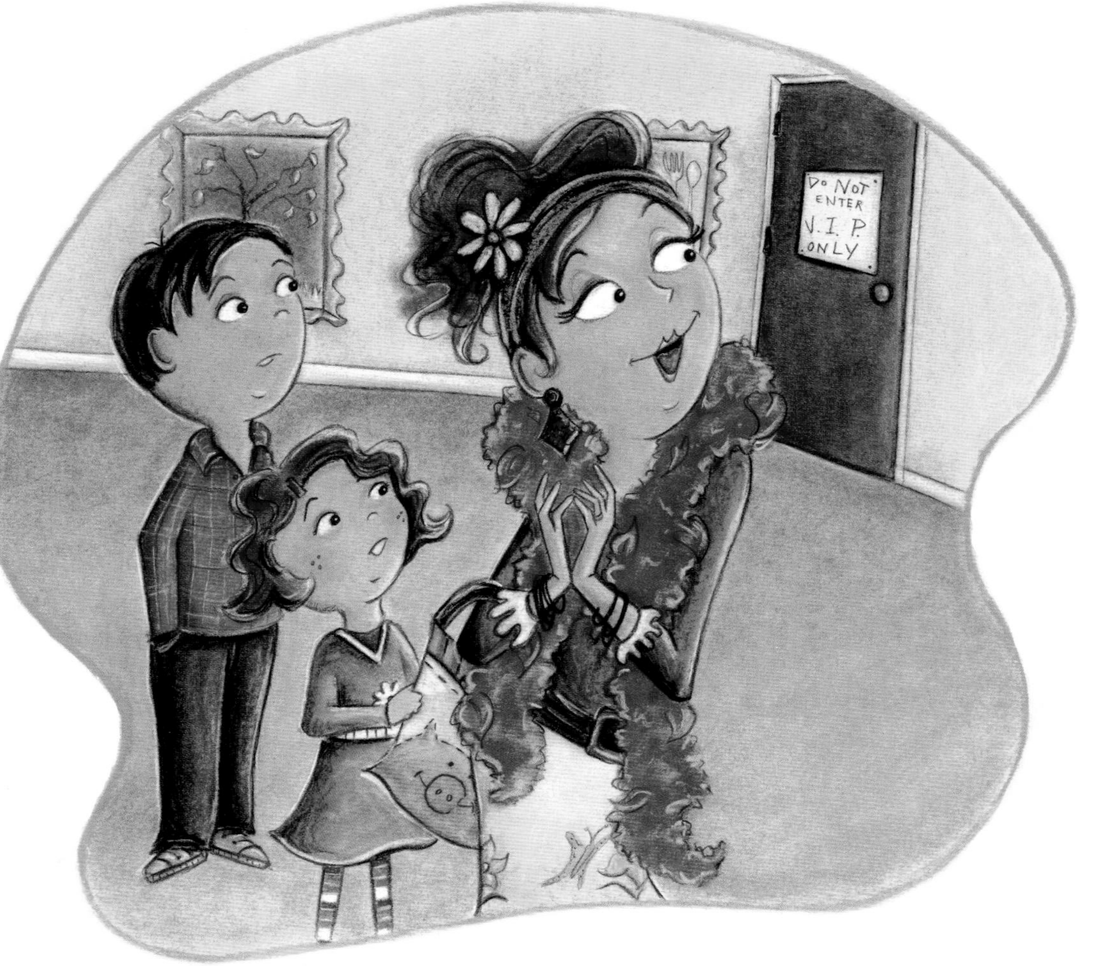
Do Not
Enter
V.I.P.
Only

Jessie tugged at her mom's sleeve. "I'm bored," she said. "There's nothing to do here but look at art! Let's go home and watch a DVD."

But their mother didn't seem to be listening. She was staring at a door on the other side of the big room.

Josh followed his mother's eyes and read the words on the door to Jessie. "Do—Not—Enter. V.I.P. Only," he read.

"What's a V.I.P.?" asked Jessie.

With a mischievous smile, Mom explained. "It stands for 'Very Important People'...like us."

Josh looked at Jessie and Jessie looked at Josh. They could sense trouble.

"No, Mom! We're not V.I.Ps," said Josh.

"We can't go in there!" added Jessie. "Let's just go home."

"Come on, kids," their mother called, heading toward the door. "Of course we're V.I.Ps! You're the most Very Important People in my life. Plus, it's an adventure!"

"No!" yelled Josh. "Mom, you promised to follow the rules!"

"Yeah! You promised!" cried Jessie.

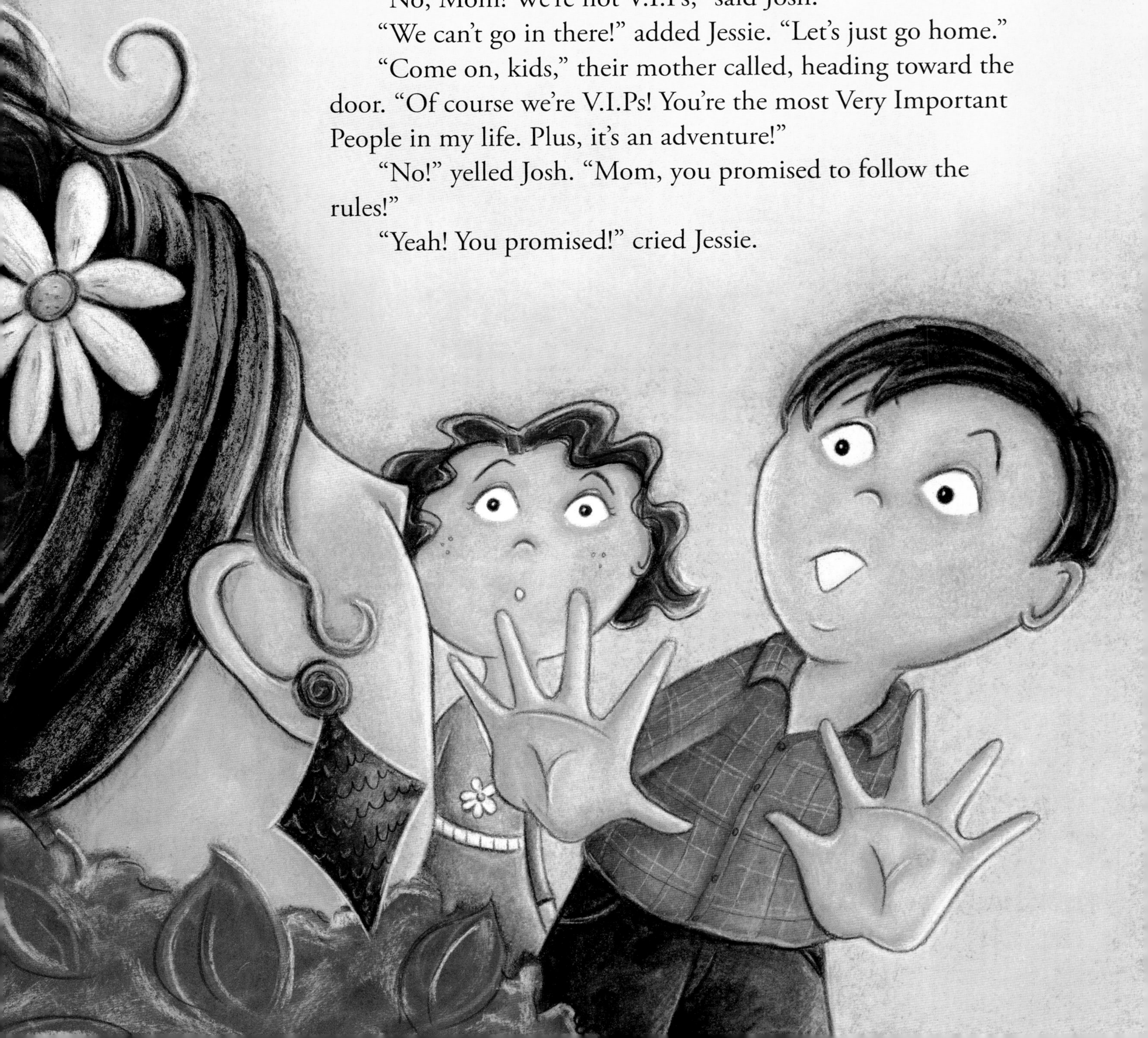

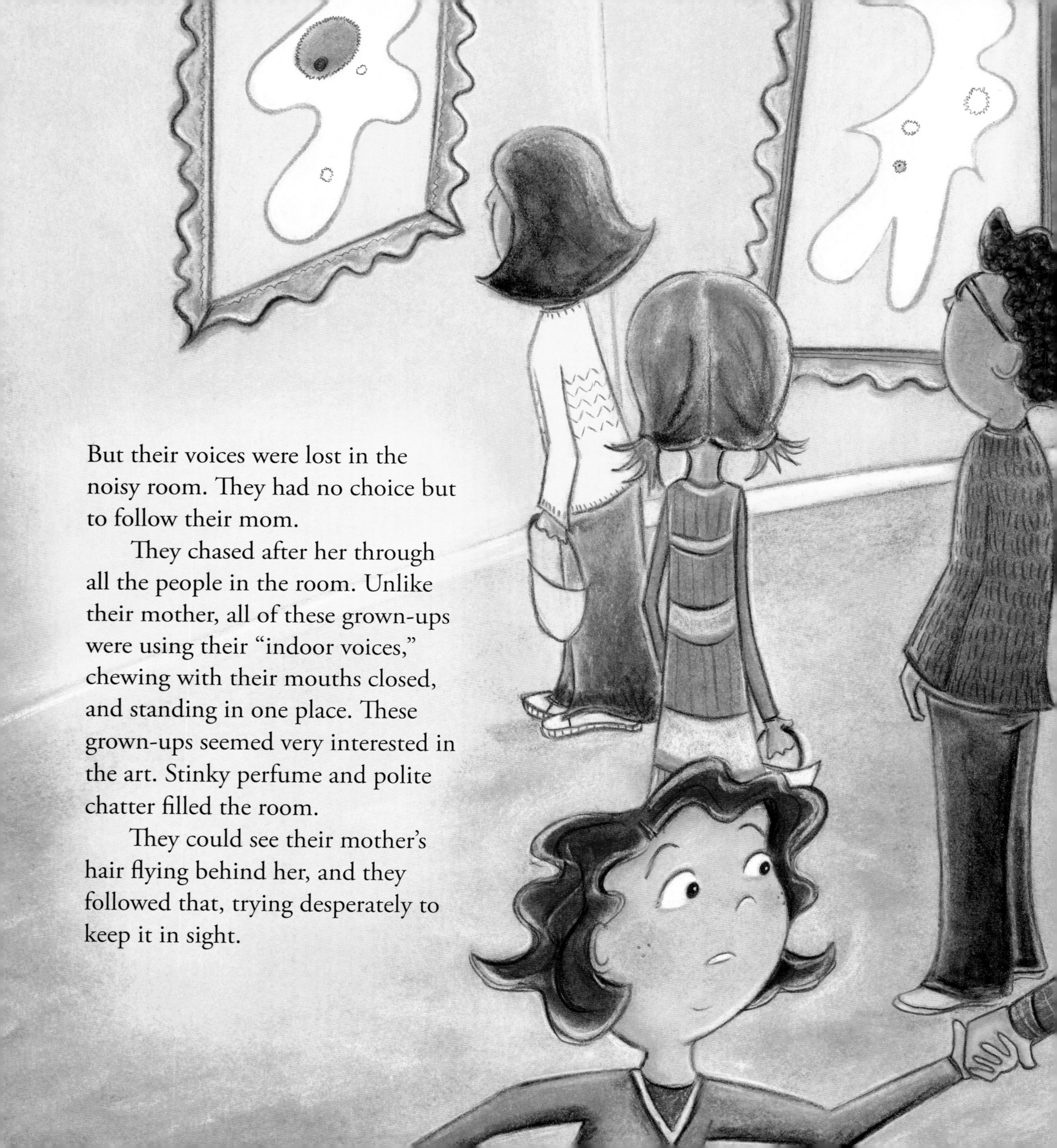

But their voices were lost in the noisy room. They had no choice but to follow their mom.

They chased after her through all the people in the room. Unlike their mother, all of these grown-ups were using their "indoor voices," chewing with their mouths closed, and standing in one place. These grown-ups seemed very interested in the art. Stinky perfume and polite chatter filled the room.

They could see their mother's hair flying behind her, and they followed that, trying desperately to keep it in sight.

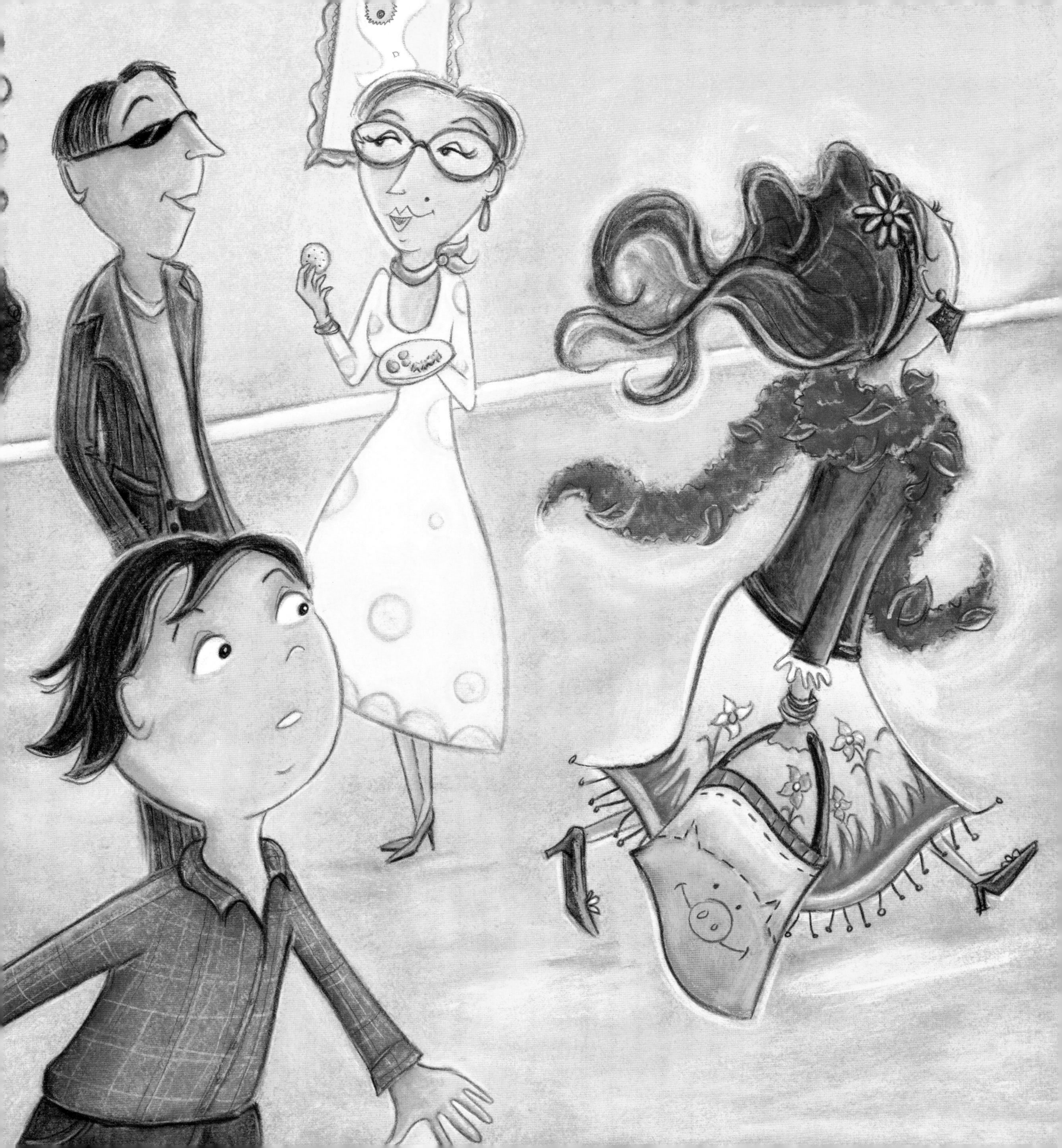

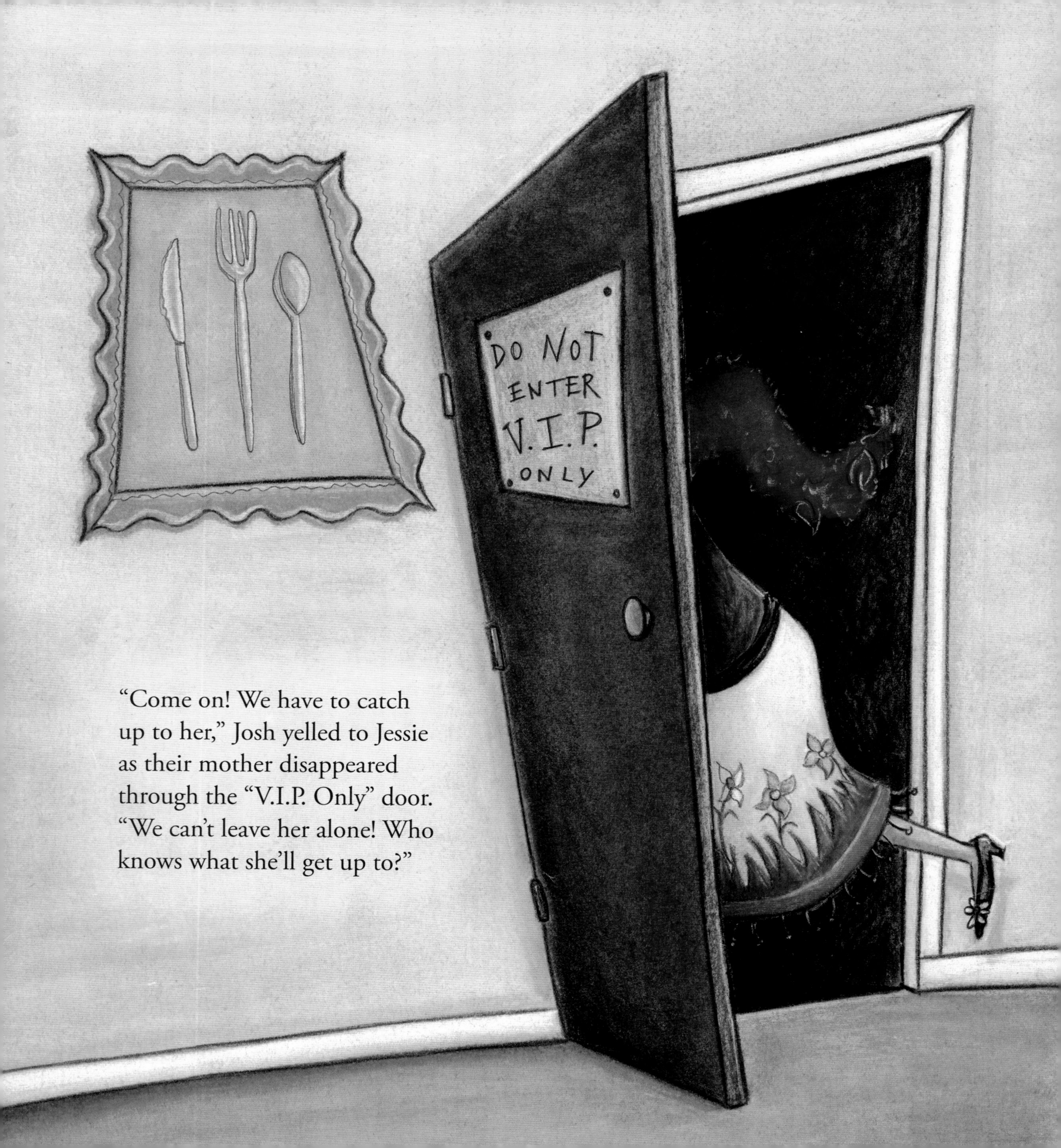
DO NOT
ENTER
V.I.P.
ONLY

"Come on! We have to catch up to her," Josh yelled to Jessie as their mother disappeared through the "V.I.P. Only" door. "We can't leave her alone! Who knows what she'll get up to?"

"You go first," said Jessie, pushing Josh forward.

He opened the door slowly. Jessie held onto his shirt.

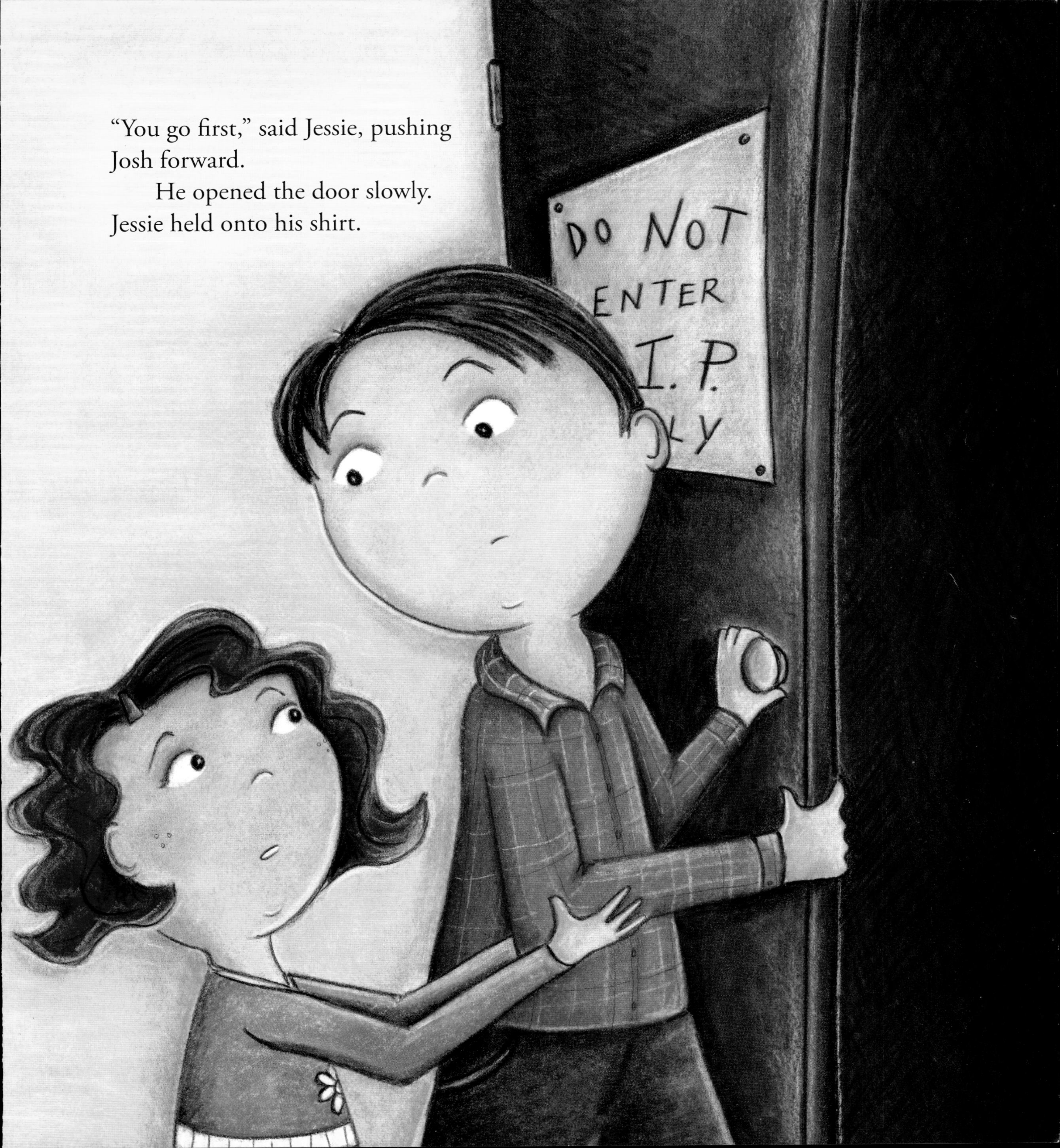
DO NOT
ENTER

The room was pitch black.
"Mom, where are you?" they yelled.

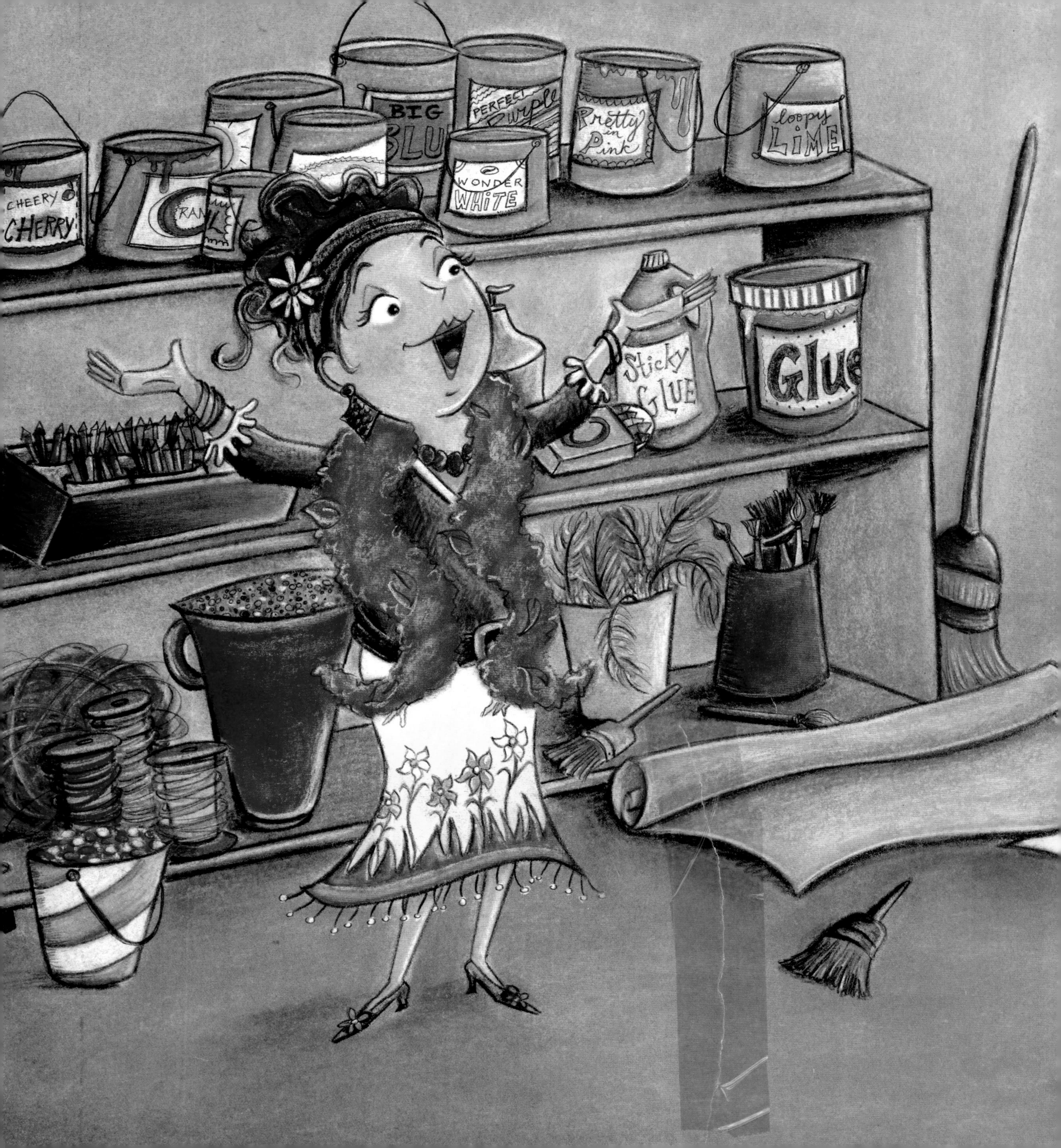
CHEERY
CHERRY
BIG
BLUE
PERFECT
Purple
WONDER
WHITE
Pretty in Pink
loopy
LIME
Sticky
GLUE
Glue

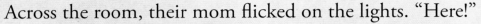

Across the room, their mom flicked on the lights. "Here!"

Jessie and Josh couldn't believe their eyes. All around them were swirls of brilliant colour. There were buckets of every shade of paint in the rainbow, pails of glue, boxes of crayons, and jars of sparkles, beads, and feathers.

"Mom, don't touch anything," Josh whispered. "We can still leave right now and no one will catch us!"

"Look at all these art supplies!" their mother said. "I want to make some art! We're at an art gallery, after all."

"Mom! I don't think you should…," Jessie started to say.

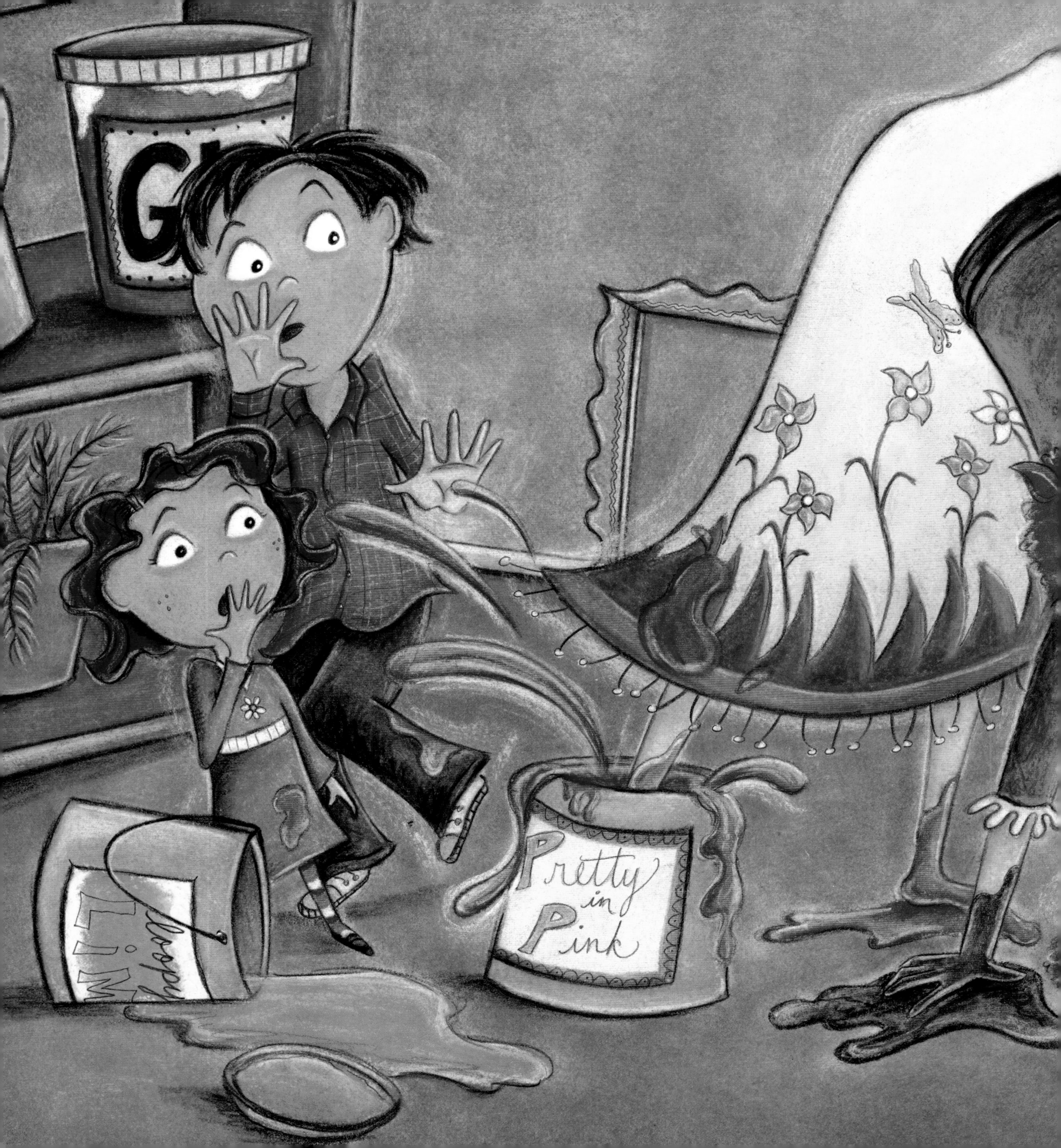
Pretty in Pink

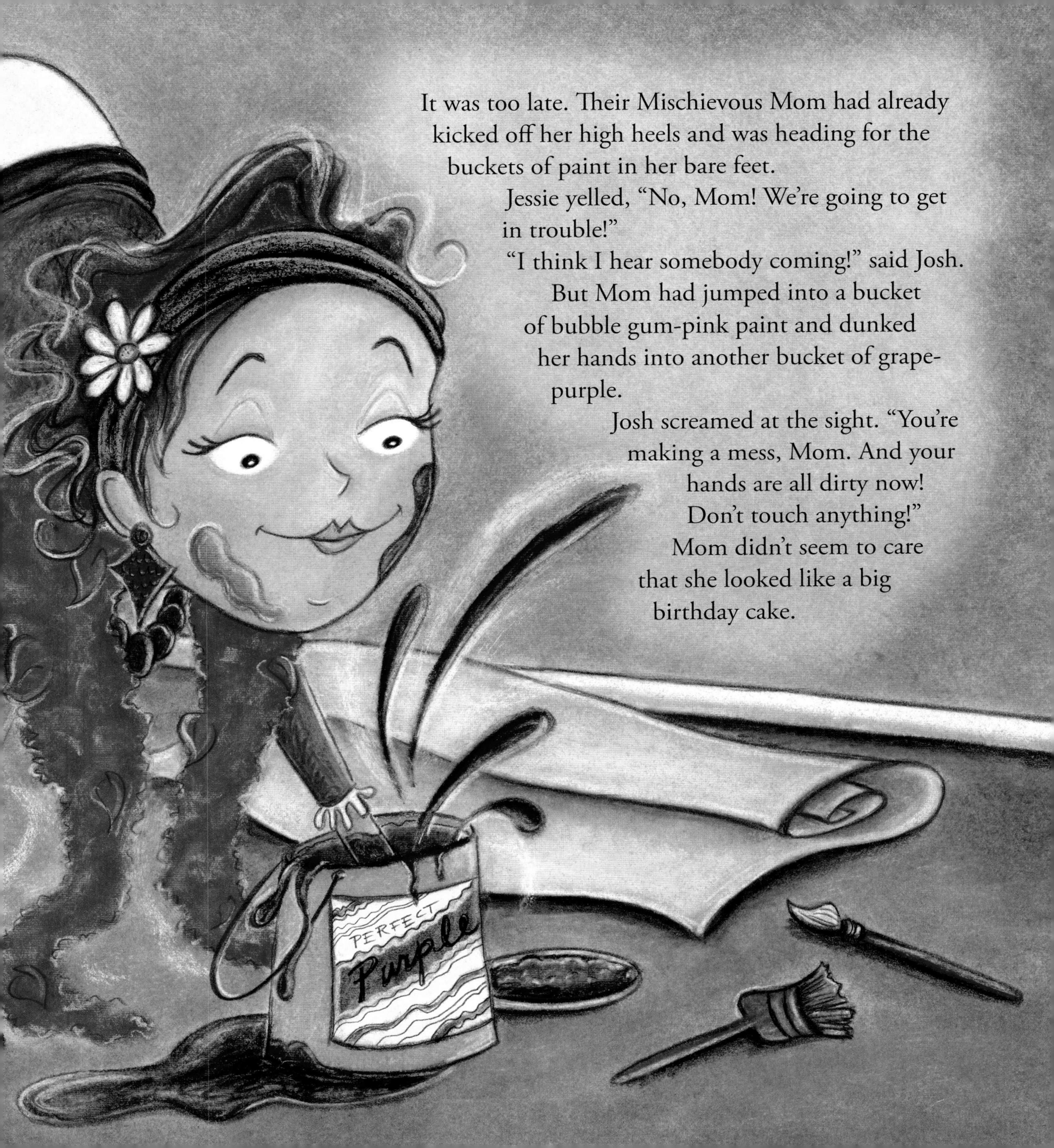
PERFECT
Purple

It was too late. Their Mischievous Mom had already kicked off her high heels and was heading for the buckets of paint in her bare feet.

Jessie yelled, “No, Mom! We’re going to get in trouble!”

“I think I hear somebody coming!” said Josh.

But Mom had jumped into a bucket of bubble gum-pink paint and dunked her hands into another bucket of grape-purple.

Josh screamed at the sight. “You’re making a mess, Mom. And your hands are all dirty now! Don’t touch anything!”

Mom didn’t seem to care that she looked like a big birthday cake.

"Come on, kids! Make some art with me!" she said, as she jumped out of the bucket, rolled out a large piece of paper, and started dancing on it, leaving footprints and handprints wherever she went.

Josh looked at Jessie and Jessie looked at Josh. It did look like so much fun.

"Okay, maybe just for a minute," said Josh.

"Yeah, just for one minute!" said Jessie.

Jessie grabbed the jar of sparkles. Josh grabbed the biggest paintbrush he'd ever seen. Before they knew it, they were all covered with paint, sparkles, feathers, and glue.

They didn't even notice how much time had gone by until they all started to yawn.

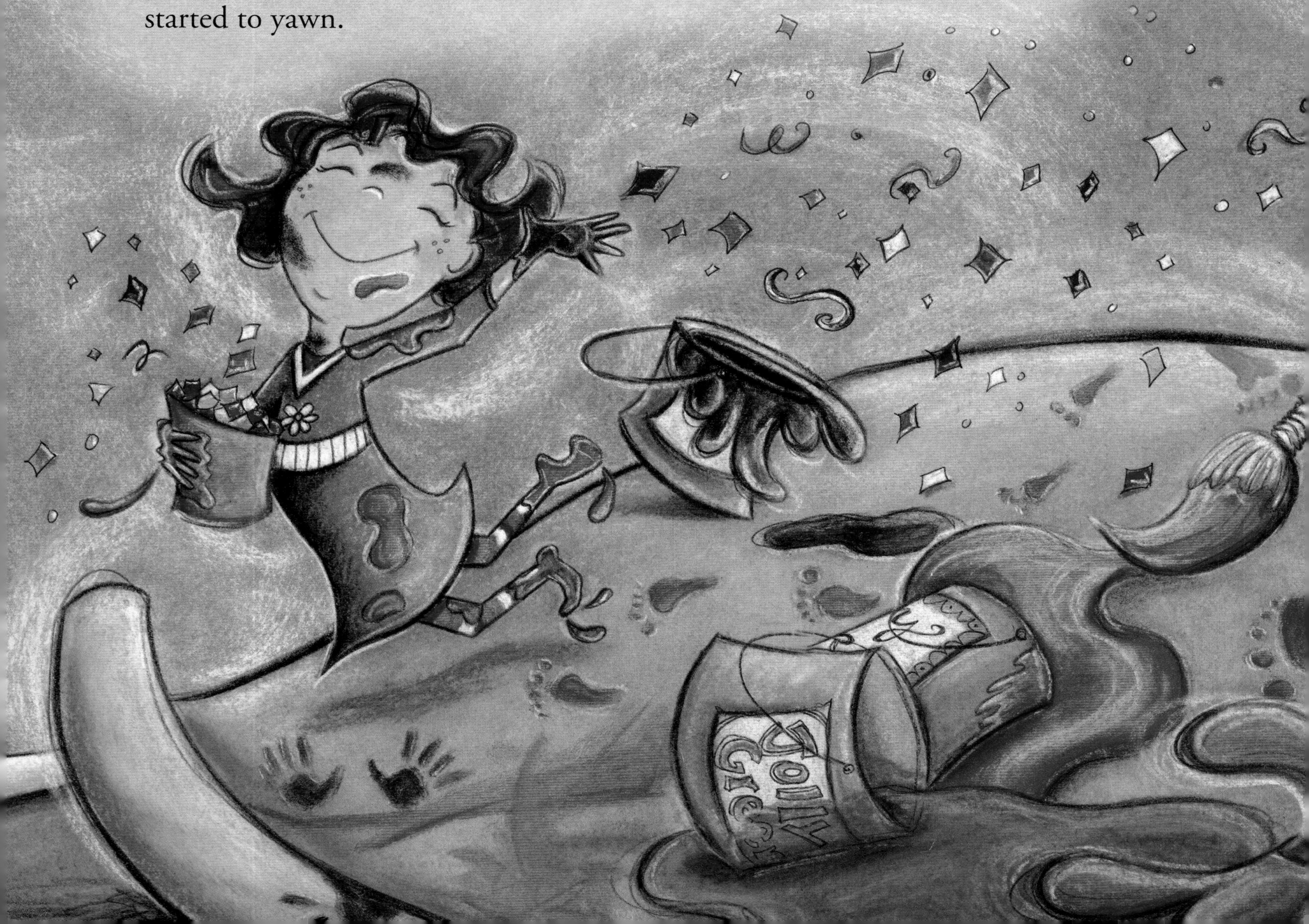

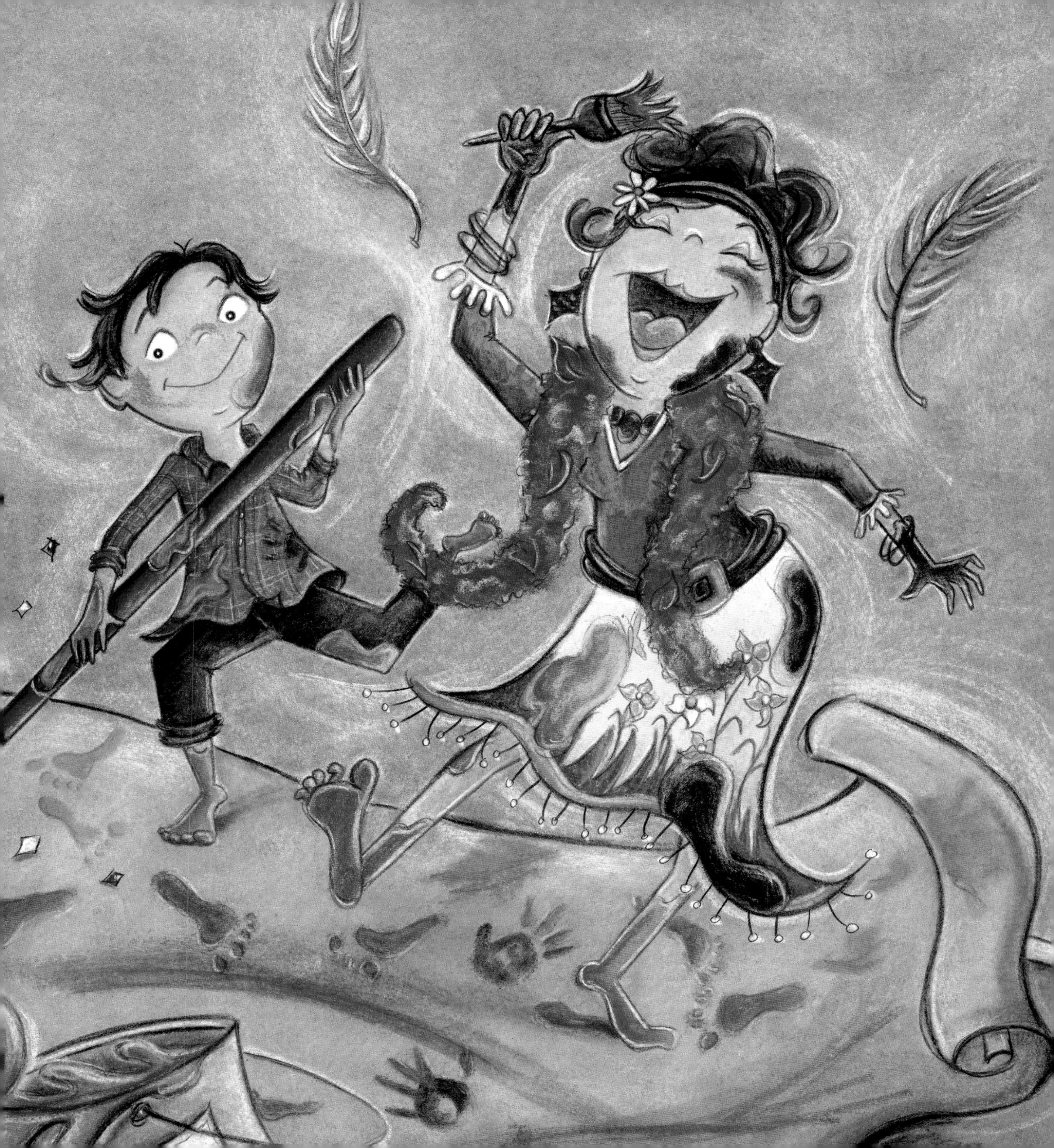

"That was the most fun I had all day," said their mother.

"Us, too!" said Jessie.

They stood back to admire their work. They all agreed it was as good as anything they had seen in the Art Gallery. Even better!

"I think it's time to go home," Mom said. "Now help me roll this up!"

They rolled up their multicoloured masterpiece, and carrying it over their shoulders, headed back through the "Do Not Enter. V.I.P. Only" door.

"Maybe we're Very Important People after all," said Josh.

"Of course we are!" said their mother.

Everyone in the gallery stared as the three messy artists headed home, leaving rainbow-coloured footprints behind.

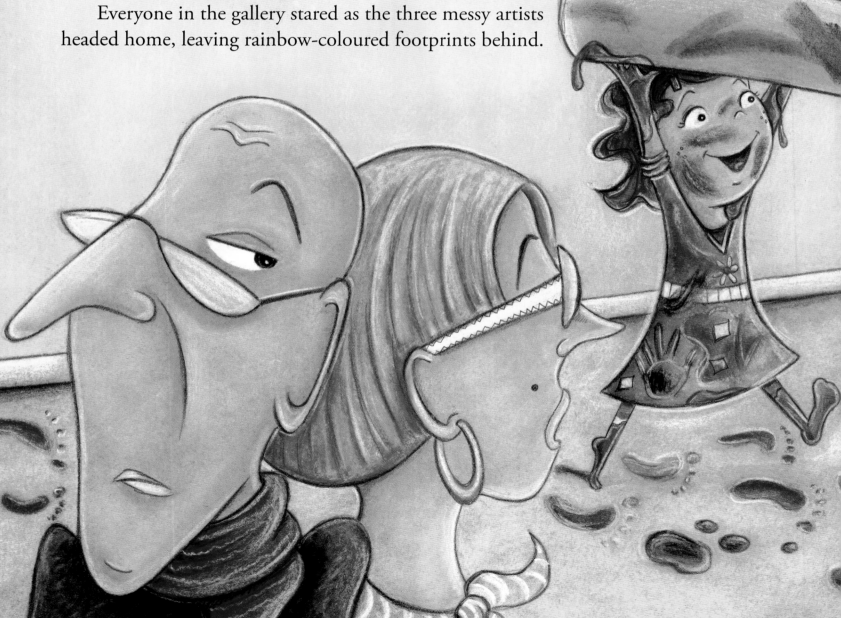

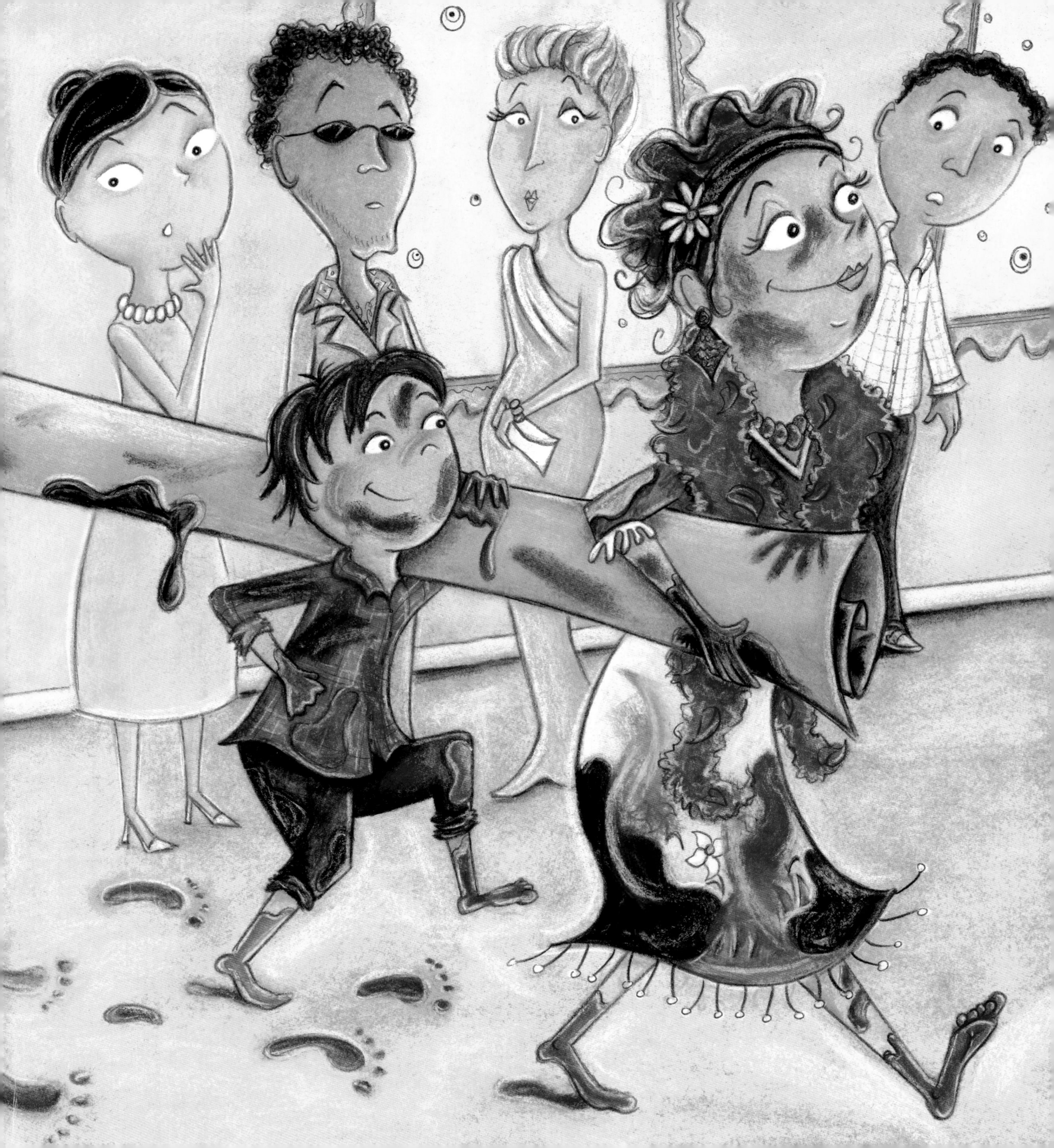

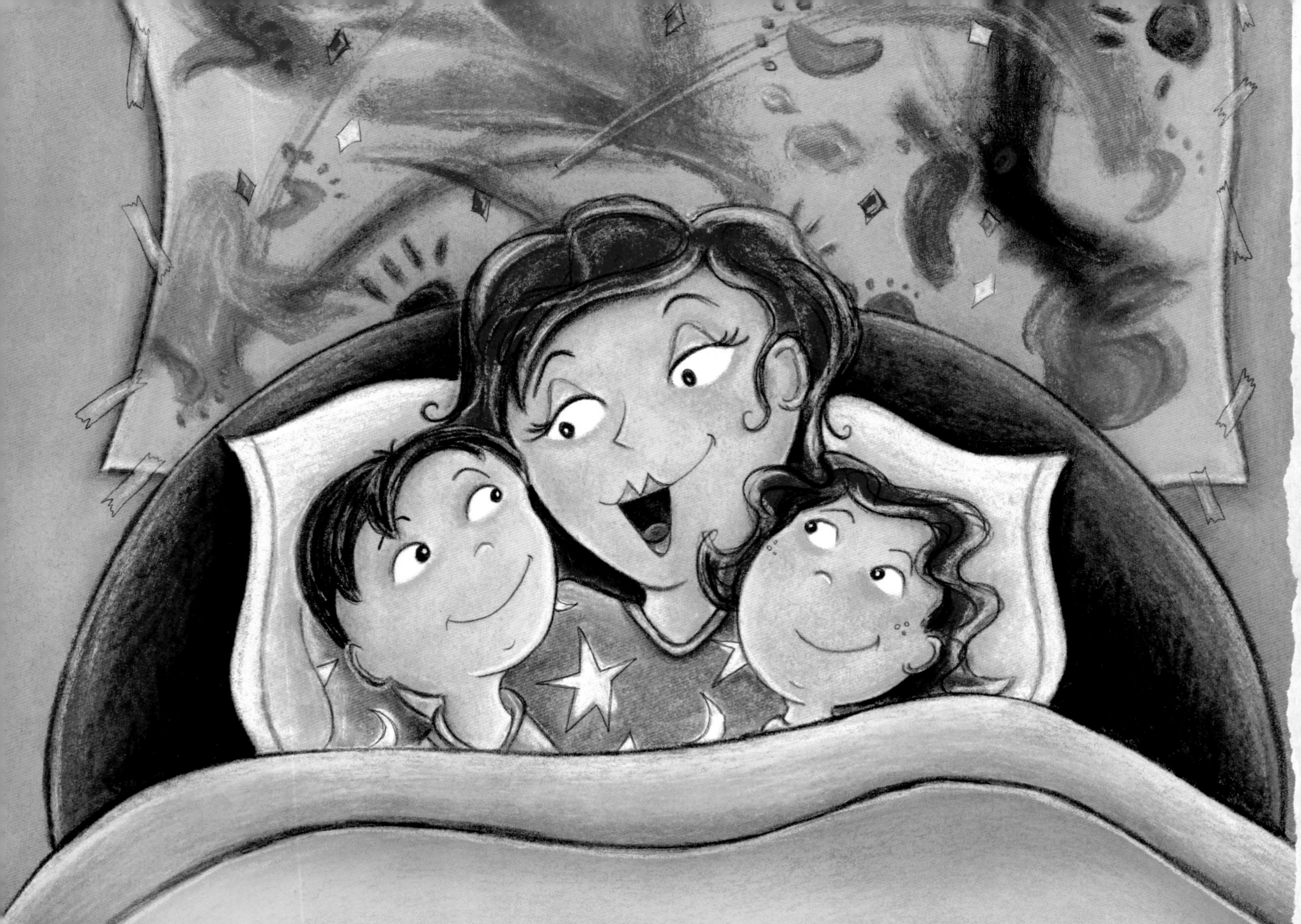

At home, after all three had long bubbles baths, brushed their teeth, and put on cozy pyjamas, it was time to be tucked into bed.

Mom climbed into her bed. She had already taped their artwork on the wall.

"Who knew an art gallery party could be so much fun?" said Josh. "But next time, Mom, you really have to follow the rules."

Mom said, "Okay, I'll try my best."

Jessie said, "Do you promise?

"I promise," said their mother. And she gave them another wink.

Jessie and Josh looked at each other. They knew better. They would always have a Mischievous Mom. And they couldn't wait until tomorrow.